michael morpurgo

THE BUTTERFLY LION

Illustrated by

CHRISTIAN BIRMINGHAM

TED SMART

For Virginia McKenna

The Butterfly Lion

"*The Butterfly Lion* tells of loneliness and love in a way that is wholly appropriate for young readers."

Julia Eccleshare, chair of adult judging panel,
Smarties Prize 1996

"A magical, mysterious story with the power to draw readers back again and again."

Jenny Morris, adult judging panel,
Smarties Prize 1996

"This beautiful story of love and war has everything – even a great twist."

Young Telegraph

"This sensitive, highly visual story deserves to be recognized as a masterpiece."

Junior Education

"The most beautifully crafted story I've read for a long time."

Wendy Cooling, *Treasure Islands*, BBC Radio 4

"Morpurgo writes with a fine mixture of clarity, depth and feeling."

Sunday Times

This edition produced for The Book People Ltd,
Hall Wood Avenue, Haydock, St Helens WA11 9UL

First published in Great Britain by Collins Children's Books 1996

26 28 30 32 34 33 31 29 27

Collins Children's Books is an imprint of HarperCollins*Publishers* Ltd,
77-85 Fulham Palace Road, Hammersmith, London W6 8JB.

The HarperCollins*Children'sBooks* website address is:
www.harpercollinschildrensbooks.co.uk

ISBN 0 00 769326 5

The author and illustrator assert the moral right to be
identified respectively as the author and illustrator of this work.

A CIP record for this title is available from the British Library.

Set in Palatino 14/21pt

Printed and bound in England by
Clays Ltd, St Ives plc

THE BUTTERFLY LION

The Butterfly Lion grew from several magical roots: the memories of a small boy who tried to run away from school a long time ago; a book about a pride of white lions discovered by Chris McBride; a chance meeting in a lift with Virginia McKenna, actress and champion of lions and all creatures born free; a true story of a soldier of the First World War who rescued some circus animals in France from certain death; and the sighting from a train of a white horse carved out on a chalky hillside near Westbury in Wiltshire.

To Chris McBride, to Virginia McKenna and to Gina Pollinger – many, many thanks. And to you the reader – enjoy it!

MICHAEL MORPURGO

February 1996

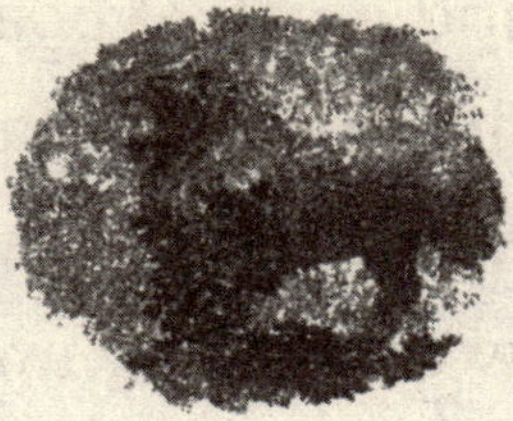

Chilblains and Semolina Pudding

Butterflies live only short lives. They flower and flutter for just a few glorious weeks, and then they die. To see them, you have to be in the right place at the right time. And that's how it was when I saw the butterfly lion – I happened to be in just the right place, at just the right time. I didn't dream him. I didn't dream any of it. I saw him, blue and shimmering in the sun, one afternoon in June when I was young. A long time ago. But I don't forget. I mustn't forget. I promised them I wouldn't.

I was ten, and away at boarding school in deepest Wiltshire. I was far from home and I didn't want to be. It was a diet of Latin and stew and rugby and detentions and cross-country runs and chilblains and marks and squeaky beds and semolina pudding. And then there was Basher Beaumont who terrorised and tormented me, so that I lived every waking moment of my life in dread of him. I had often thought of running away, but only once ever plucked up the courage to do it.

I was homesick after a letter from my mother. Basher Beaumont had cornered me in the bootroom and smeared black shoe-polish in my hair. I had done badly in a spelling test, and Mr Carter had stood me in the corner with a book on my head all through the lesson – his favourite torture. I was more miserable than I had ever been before. I picked at the plaster in the wall, and determined there and then that I would run away.

I took off the next Sunday afternoon. With any luck I wouldn't be missed till supper, and by that time I'd be home, home and free. I climbed the fence at the bottom of the school park, behind the trees where I couldn't be seen. Then I ran for it. I ran as if bloodhounds were after me, not stopping till I was through Innocents Breach and out onto the road beyond. I had my escape all planned. I would walk to the station – it was only five miles or so – and catch the train to London. Then I'd take the underground home. I'd just walk in and tell them that I was never, ever going back.

There wasn't much traffic, but all the same I turned up the collar of my raincoat so that no one could catch a glimpse of my uniform. It was beginning to rain now, those heavy hard drops that mean there's

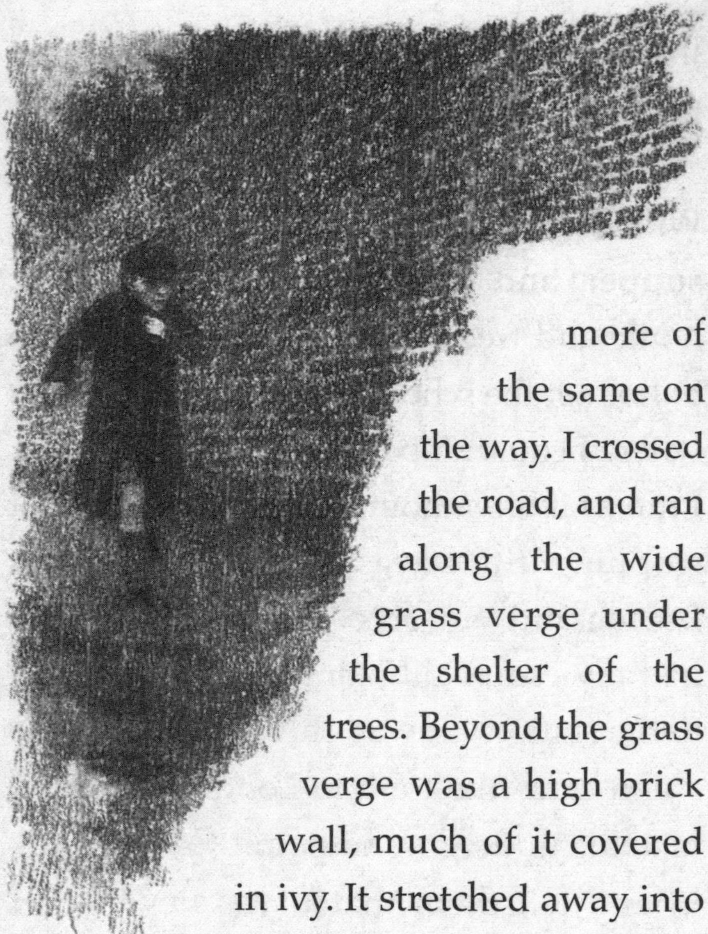

more of the same on the way. I crossed the road, and ran along the wide grass verge under the shelter of the trees. Beyond the grass verge was a high brick wall, much of it covered in ivy. It stretched away into the distance, continuous as far as the eye could see, except for a massive arched gateway at the bend of the road. A great stone lion bestrode the gateway. As I came closer I could see he was roaring in the rain, his lip curled, his teeth bared.

I stopped and stared up at him for a moment. That was when I heard a car slowing down behind me. I did not think twice. I pushed open the iron gate, darted through, and flattened myself behind the stone pillar. I watched the car until it disappeared round the bend.

To be caught would mean a caning, four strokes, maybe six, across the back of the knees. Worse, I would be back at school, back to detentions, back to Basher Beaumont. To go along the road was dangerous, too dangerous. I would try to cut across country to the station. It would be longer that way, but far safer.

Strange Meeting

I was still deciding which direction to take when I heard a voice from behind me.

"Who are you? What do you want?"

I turned.

"Who are you?" she asked again. The old lady who stood before me was no bigger than I was. She scrutinised me from under the shadow of her dripping straw hat. She had piercing dark eyes that I did not want to look into.

"I didn't think it would rain," she said, her voice gentler. "Lost, are you?"

I said nothing. She had a dog on a leash at her side, a big dog. There was an ominous growl in his throat, and his hackles were up all along his back.

She smiled. "The dog says you're on private property," she went on, pointing her stick at me accusingly. She edged aside my raincoat with the end of her stick. "Run away from that school, did you? Well, if it's anything like it used to be, I can't say I blame you. But we can't just stand here in the rain, can we? You'd better come inside. We'll give him some tea, shall we, Jack? Don't you worry about Jack. He's all bark and no bite." Looking at Jack, I found that hard to believe.

I don't know why, but I never for one moment thought of running off. I often wondered later why I went with her so readily. I think it was because she expected me to, willed me to somehow. I followed the old lady and her dog up to the house, which was huge, as huge as my school. It looked as if it had grown out of the ground.

There was hardly a brick or a stone or a tile to be seen. The entire building was smothered in red creeper, and there were a dozen ivy-clad chimneys sprouting skywards from the roof.

We sat down close to the stove in a vast vaulted kitchen. "The kitchen's always the warmest place," she said, opening the oven door. "We'll have you dry in no time. Scones?" she went on, bending down with some difficulty and reaching inside. "I always have scones on a Sunday. And tea to wash it down. All right for you?" She went on chatting away as she busied herself with the kettle and the teapot. The dog eyed me all the while from his basket, unblinking. "I was just thinking," she said. "You'll be the first young man I've had inside this house since Bertie." She was silent for a while.

The smell of the scones wafted through the kitchen. I ate three before I even touched my tea. They were sweet and crumbly,

and succulent with melting butter. She talked on merrily again, to me, to the dog – I wasn't sure which. I wasn't really listening. I was looking out of the window behind her. The sun was bursting through the clouds and lighting the hillside. A perfect rainbow arched through the sky. But miraculous though it was, it wasn't the rainbow that fascinated me. Somehow, the clouds were casting a strange shadow over the hillside, a shadow the shape of a lion, roaring like the one over the archway.

"Sun's come out," said the old lady, offering me another scone. I took it eagerly. "Always does, you know. It may be difficult to remember sometimes, but there's always sun behind the clouds, and the clouds do go in the end. Honestly."

She watched me eat, a smile on her face that warmed me to the bone.

"Don't think I want you to go, because I don't. Nice to see a boy eat so well, nice to have the company; but all the same, I'd better get you back to school after you've had your tea, hadn't I? You'll only be in trouble otherwise. Mustn't run off, you know. You've got to stick it out, see things through, do what's got to be done, no matter what." She was looking out of the window as she spoke. "My Bertie taught me that, bless him, or maybe I taught him. I can't remember now." And she went on talking and talking, but my mind was elsewhere again.

The lion on the hillside was still there, but now he was blue and shimmering in the sunlight. It was as if he were breathing, as if he were alive. It wasn't a shadow any more. No shadow is blue. "No, you're not seeing things," the old lady whispered. "It's not magic. He's real enough. He's our lion, Bertie's and mine. He's our butterfly lion."

"What d'you mean?" I asked.

She looked at me long and hard. "I'll tell you if you like," she said. "Would you like to know? Would you really like to know?"

I nodded.

"Have another scone first and another cup of tea. Then I'll take you to Africa where our lion came from, where my Bertie came from too. Bit of a story, I can tell you. You ever been to Africa?"

"No," I replied.

"Well, you're going," she said. "We're both going."

Suddenly I wasn't hungry any more. All I wanted now was to hear her story. She sat back in her chair, gazing out of the window. She told it slowly, thinking before each sentence; and all the while she never took her eyes off the butterfly lion. And neither did I.

Timbavati

Bertie was born in South Africa, in a remote farmhouse near a place called Timbavati. It was shortly after Bertie first started to walk that his mother and father decided a fence must be put around the farmhouse to make a compound where Bertie could play in safety. It wouldn't keep the snakes out – nothing could do that – but at least Bertie would be safe now from the leopards, and the lions and the spotted hyenas. Enclosed within the compound were the lawn and gardens at the front of the house, and the stables and barns at the back – all the room a child would need or want, you might think. But not Bertie.

The farm stretched as far as the eye could see in all directions, twenty thousand acres of veld. Bertie's father farmed cattle, but times were hard. The rains had failed too often, and many of the rivers and waterholes had all but dried up. With fewer wildebeest and impala to prey on, the lions and leopards would sneak up on the cattle whenever they could. So Bertie's father was more often than not away from home with his men, guarding the cattle. Every time he left, he'd say the same thing: "Don't you ever open that gate, Bertie, you hear me? There's lions out there, leopards, elephants, hyenas. You stay put, you hear?" Bertie would stand at the fence and watch him ride out, and he would be left behind with his mother, who was also his teacher. There were no schools for a hundred miles. And his mother too was always warning him to stay inside the fence. "Look what happened in *Peter and the Wolf*," she would say.

His mother was often sick with malaria, and even when she wasn't sick she would be listless and sad. There were good days, days when she would play the piano for him and play hide-and-seek around the compound. Or he'd sit on her lap on the sofa out on the veranda and she'd just talk and talk, all about her home in England, about how much she hated the wildness and the loneliness of Africa, and about how Bertie was everything to her.

But they were rare days. Every morning he'd climb into her bed and snuggle up to her, hoping against hope that today she'd be well and happy; but so often she wasn't, and Bertie would be left on his own again, to his own devices.

There was a waterhole downhill from the farmhouse, and some distance away. That waterhole, when there was water in it, became Bertie's whole world. He would spend hours in the dusty compound, his hands gripping the fence, looking out at the wonders of the veld, at the giraffes

drinking, spread-legged, at the waterhole; at the browsing impala, tails twitching, alert; at the warthogs snorting and snuffling under the shade of the shingayi trees; at the baboons, the zebras, the wildebeests, and the elephants bathing in the mud. But the moment Bertie always longed for was when a pride of lions came padding out of the veld. The impala were the first to spring away, then the zebra would panic and gallop off. Within seconds the lions would have the waterhole to themselves, and they would crouch to drink.

From the safe haven of the compound Bertie looked and learned as he grew up. By now, he could climb the tree by the farmhouse, and sit high in its branches. He could see better from up there. He would wait for his lions for hours on end. He got to know the life of the waterhole so well that he could feel the lions were out there, even before he saw them.

Bertie had no friends to play with, but he always said he was never lonely as a child. At night he loved reading his books and losing himself in the stories, and by day his heart was out in the veld with the animals. That was where he yearned to be. Whenever his mother was well enough, he would beg her to take him outside the compound, but her answer was always the same.

"I can't, Bertie. Your father has forbidden it," she'd say. And that was that.

The men would come home with their stories of the veld, of the family of cheetahs sitting like sentinels on their kopje, of the leopard they had spotted high in his tree larder watching over his kill, of the hyenas they had driven off, of the herd of elephants which had stampeded the cattle. And Bertie would listen wide-eyed, agog. Again and again he asked his father if he could go with him to help guard the cattle. His father just laughed, patted his head, and said it was man's work. He did teach Bertie how to ride, and how to shoot too, but always within the confines of the compound.

Week in, week out, Bertie had to stay behind his fence. He made up his mind though, that if no one would take him out into the veld, then one day he would go by himself. But something always held him back. Perhaps it was one of those tales he'd been told of black mamba snakes whose bite would kill you within ten minutes, of hyenas whose jaws would crunch you to bits, of vultures who would finish off anything that was left so that no one would ever find even the bits. For the time being he stayed behind the fence. But the more he grew up, the more his compound became a prison to him.

One evening – Bertie must have been about six years old by now – he was sitting high up in the branches of his tree, hoping against hope the lions might come down for their sunset drink as they often did. He was thinking of giving up, for it would soon be too dark to see much now, when he saw a solitary lioness come down to the waterhole. Then he saw that she was not alone. Behind her, and on unsteady legs, came what looked like a lion cub – but it was white, glowing white in the gathering gloom of dusk.

While the lioness drank, the cub played at catching her tail; and then, when she had had her fill, the two of them slipped away into the long grass and were gone.

Bertie ran inside, screaming with excitement. He had to tell someone, anyone. He found his father working at his desk.

"Impossible," said his father. "You're seeing things that aren't there, or you're telling fibs – one of the two."

"I saw him. I promise," Bertie insisted. But his father would have none of it, and sent him to his room for arguing.

His mother came to see him later. "Anyone can make a mistake, Bertie dear," she said. "It must have been the sunset. It plays tricks with your eyes sometimes. There's no such thing as a white lion."

The next evening Bertie watched again at the fence, but the white lion cub and the lioness did not come, nor did they the next evening, nor the next. Bertie began to think he must have been dreaming it.

A week or more passed, and there had been only a few zebras and wildebeest down at the waterhole. Bertie was already upstairs in his bed when he heard his father riding into the compound, and then the stamp of his heavy boots on the veranda.

"We got her! We got her!" he was saying. "Huge lioness, massive she was.

She's taken half a dozen of my best cattle in the last two weeks. Well, she won't be taking any more."

Bertie's heart stopped. In that one terrible moment he knew which lioness his father was talking about. There could be no doubt about it. His white lion cub had been orphaned.

"But what if," Bertie's mother was saying, "what if she had young ones to feed? Perhaps they were starving."

"So would we be if we let it go on. We had to shoot her," his father retorted.

Bertie lay there all night listening to the plaintive roaring echoing through the veld, as if every lion in Africa was sounding a lament. He turned his face into his pillow and could think of nothing but the orphaned white cub, and he promised himself there and then that if ever the cub came down to the waterhole looking for his dead mother, then he would do what he had never dared to do, he would open the gate and go out and bring him home. He would not let him die out there all alone. But no lion cub came to his waterhole. All day, every day, he waited for him to come, but he never came.

Bertie and the Lion

One morning, a week or so later, Bertie was woken by a chorus of urgent neighing. He jumped out of his bed and ran to the window. A herd of zebras was scattering away from the waterhole, chased by a couple of hyenas. Then he saw more hyenas, three of them, standing stock still, noses pointing, eyes fixed on the waterhole. It was only now that Bertie saw the lion cub. But this one wasn't white at all. He was covered in mud, with his back to the waterhole, and he was waving a pathetic paw at the hyenas who were beginning to circle. The lion cub had nowhere to run to, and the hyenas were sidling ever closer.

Bertie was downstairs in a flash, leaping off the veranda and racing barefoot across the compound, shouting at the top of his voice. He threw open the gate and charged down the hill towards the waterhole, yelling and screaming and waving his arms like a wild thing. Startled at this sudden intrusion, the hyenas turned tail and ran, but not far. Once within range Bertie hurled a broadside of pebbles at them, and they ran off again, but again not far. Then he was at the waterhole and between the lion cub and the hyenas, shouting at them to go away. They didn't. They stood and watched, uncertain for a while. Then they began to circle again, closer, closer…

That was when the shot rang out. The hyenas bolted into the long grass, and were gone. When Bertie turned round he saw his mother in her nightgown, rifle in hand, running towards him down the hill.

He had never seen her run before. Between them they gathered up the mud-matted cub and brought him home. He was too weak to struggle, though he tried. As soon as they had given him some warm milk, they dunked him in the bath to wash him. As the first of the mud came off, Bertie saw he was white underneath.

"You see!" he cried triumphantly. "He *is* white! He *is*. I told you, didn't I? He's my white lion!" His mother still could not bring herself to believe it. Five baths later, she had to.

They sat him down by the stove in a washing basket and fed him again, all the milk he could drink, and he drank the lot. Then he lay down and slept. He was still asleep when Bertie's father got back at lunch time. They told him how it had all happened.

"Please, Father. I want to keep him," Bertie said.

"And so do I," said his mother. "We both do." And she spoke as Bertie had never heard her speak before, her voice strong, determined.

Bertie's father didn't seem to know quite how to reply. He just said: "We'll talk about it later," and then he walked out.

They did talk about it later when Bertie was supposed to be in bed. He wasn't, though. He heard them arguing. He was outside the sitting-room door, watching, listening. His father was pacing up and down.

"He'll grow up, you know," he was saying. "You can't keep a grown lion, you know that."

"And *you* know we can't just throw him to the hyenas," replied his mother. "He needs us, and maybe we need him. He'll be someone for Bertie to play with for a while." And then she added sadly: "After all, it's not as if he's going to have any brothers and sisters, is it?"

At this, Bertie's father went over to her and kissed her gently on the forehead. It was the only time Bertie had ever seen him kiss her.

"All right then," he said. "All right. You can keep your lion."

So the white lion cub came to live amongst them in the farmhouse. He slept at the end of Bertie's bed. Wherever Bertie went, the lion cub went too – even to the bathroom, where he would watch Bertie have his bath and lick his legs dry afterwards. They were never apart. It was Bertie who saw to the feeding – milk four times a day from one of his father's beer bottles – until later on when the lion cub lapped from a soup bowl. There was impala meat whenever he wanted it, and as he grew – and he grew fast – he wanted more and more of it.

For the first time in his life Bertie was totally happy. The lion cub was all the brothers and sisters he could ever want, all the friends he could ever need. The two of them would sit side by side on the sofa out on the veranda and watch the great red sun go down over Africa, and Bertie would read him *Peter and the Wolf*, and at the end he would always promise him that he would never let him go off to a zoo and live behind bars like the wolf in the story. And the lion cub would look up at Bertie with his trusting amber eyes.

"Why don't you give him a name?" his mother asked one day.

"Because he doesn't need one," replied Bertie. "He's a lion, not a person. Lions don't need names."

Bertie's mother was always wonderfully patient with the lion, no matter how much mess he made, how many cushions he pounced on and ripped apart, no matter how much crockery he smashed. None of it seemed to upset her. And strangely, she was hardly ever ill these days. There was a spring to her step, and her laughter pealed around the house. His father was less happy about it. "Lions," he'd mutter on, "should not live in houses. You should keep him outside in the compound." But they never did. For both mother and son, the lion had brought new life to their days, life and laughter.

Running Free

It was the best year of Bertie's young life. But when it ended, it ended more painfully than he could ever have imagined. He'd always known that one day when he was older he would have to go away to school, but he had thought and hoped it would not be for a long time yet. He'd simply put it out of his mind.

His father had just returned home from Johannesburg after his yearly business trip. He broke the news at supper that first evening. Bertie knew there was something in the wind. His mother had been sad again in recent days, not sick, just strangely sad. She wouldn't look him in the eye and she winced whenever she tried to smile at him. The lion had just lain down beside him, his head warm on Bertie's feet, when his father cleared his throat and began. It was going to be a lecture. Bertie had had them before often enough, about manners, about being truthful, about the dangers of leaving the compound.

"You'll soon be eight, Bertie," he said. "And your mother and I have been doing some thinking. A boy needs a proper education, a good school. Well, we've found just the right place for you, a school near Salisbury in England. Your Uncle George and Aunt Melanie live nearby and have promised to look after you in the holidays, and to visit you from time to time. They'll be father and mother to you for a while. You'll get on with them well enough, I'm sure you will. They are fine, good people. So you'll be off on the ship to England in

July. Your mother will accompany you. She will spend the summer with you in Salisbury, and after she has taken you to your school in September, she'll then return here to the farm. It's all arranged."

As his heart filled with a terrible dread, all Bertie could think of was his white lion. "But the lion," he cried, "what about the lion?"

"I'm afraid there's something else I have to tell you," his father said. Looking across at Bertie's mother, he took a deep breath. And then he told him. He told him he had met a man whilst he was in Johannesburg, a Frenchman, a circus owner from France. He was over in Africa looking for lions and elephants to buy for his circus. He liked them young, very young, a year or less, so that he could train them up without too much trouble. Besides, they were easier and cheaper to transport when they were young. He would be coming out to the farm in a few days' time to see the white lion for himself. If he liked what he saw, he would pay good money and take him away.

It was the only time in his life Bertie had ever shouted at his father. "No! No, you can't!" It was rage that wrung the hot tears from him, but they soon gave way to silent tears of sadness and loss. There was no comforting him, but his mother tried all the same.

"We can't keep him here for ever, Bertie," she said. "We always knew that, didn't we? And you've seen how he stands by the fence gazing out into the veld. You've seen him pacing up and down. But we can't just let him out. He'd be all on his own, no mother to protect him. He couldn't cope. He'd be dead in weeks. You know he would."

"But you can't send him to a circus! You can't!" said Bertie. "He'll be shut up behind bars. I promised him he never would be. And they'll point at him. They'll laugh at him. He'd rather die. Any animal would." But he knew as he looked across the table at them that it was hopeless, that their minds were quite made up.

For Bertie the betrayal was total. That night he made up his mind what had to be done. He waited until he heard his father's deep breathing next door. Then, with his white lion at his heels, he crept downstairs in his pyjamas, took down his father's rifle from the rack and stepped out into the night. The compound gate yawned open noisily when he pushed it, but then they were out, out and running free. Bertie had no thought of the dangers around him, only that he must get as far from home as he could before he did it.

The lion padded along beside him, stopping every now and again to sniff the air. A clump of trees became a herd of elephants wandering towards them out of the dawn. Bertie ran for it. He knew how elephants hated lions. He ran and ran till his legs could run no more. As the sun came up over the veld he climbed to the top of a kopje and sat down, his arm round the lion's neck. The time had come.

"Be wild now," he whispered. "You've got to be wild. Don't come home. Don't ever come home. They'll put you behind bars. You hear what I'm saying? All my life I'll think of you, I promise I will. I won't ever forget you." And he buried his head in the lion's neck and heard the greeting groan from deep inside him. He stood up. "I'm going now," he said. "Don't follow me. Please don't follow me." And Bertie clambered down off the kopje and walked away.

When he looked back, the lion was still sitting there watching him; but then he stood up, yawned, stretched, licked his lips and sprang down after him. Bertie shouted at him, but he kept coming. He threw sticks. He threw stones. Nothing worked. The lion would stop, but then as soon as Bertie walked on, he simply followed at a safe distance.

"Go back!" Bertie yelled, "you stupid, stupid lion! I hate you! I hate you! Go back!" But the lion kept loping after him whatever he did, whatever he said.

There was only one thing for it. He didn't want to do it, but he had to. With tears filling his eyes and his mouth, he lifted the rifle to his shoulder and fired over the lion's head. At once the lion turned tail and scampered away through the veld. Bertie fired again. He watched till he could see him no more, and then turned for home. He knew he'd have to face what was coming to him. Maybe his father would strap him – he'd threatened it often enough – but Bertie didn't mind. His lion would have his chance for freedom, maybe not much of one. Anything was better than the bars and whips of a circus.

The Frenchman

They were there waiting on the veranda, his mother in her nightgown, his father in his hat, his horse saddled, ready to come after him. "I've set him free," Bertie cried. "I've set him free, so he won't ever have to live behind bars." He was sent to his room at once, where he threw himself on his bed and buried his face in his pillow.

Day after day his father went out looking for the white lion, but each evening he came back empty-handed and blazing with fury.

"What'll I tell the Frenchman when he comes, eh? Did you for one minute think of that, Bertie? Did you? I should strap you. Any father worth his salt would strap you." But he didn't.

Bertie spent all day and every day at the fence, or up his tree in the compound, or at his bedroom window, his eyes scanning the veld for anything white moving through the grass. He prayed at his bedside every night until his knees were numb, prayed that his white lion would learn how to kill, would somehow find enough to eat, would avoid the hyenas, and other lions too, come to that. Above all, he prayed he would not come back, at least not until the Frenchman from the circus had come and gone.

The day the Frenchman came, it rained, the first rain for months, it seemed. Bertie watched him as he stood there, dripping on the veranda, his thumb hooked into his waistcoat pocket, as Bertie's father broke the news that there was no white lion to collect, that he had escaped. That was the moment when Bertie's mother put her hand to her throat, cried out and pointed. The white lion was wandering through the open compound gate, yowling pitifully. Bertie ran to him and fell on his knees and held him. The lion was soaked to the skin and trembling. He was panting with hunger and so thin that you could see his rib cage. They all helped to rub him down, and then looked on as he ate ravenously.

"*Incroyable*! *Magnifique*!" said the Frenchman. "And white, just as you said, white like the snow, and tame too. He will be the star of my circus. I shall call him *'Le Prince Blanc'*, 'The White Prince'. He will have all he needs, all he wants, fresh meat every day, fresh straw every night. I love my animals, you know. They are my family, and this lion of yours, he will be my favourite son. Have no fear, young man, I promise you that he will never be hungry again." He put his hand on his heart. "As God is my witness, I promise it."

Bertie looked up into the Frenchman's face. It was a kind face, not smiling, yet earnest and trustworthy. But even so, it did not make Bertie feel any better.

"There, you see," said Bertie's mother. "He'll be happy, and that's all that matters, Bertie, isn't it?"

Bertie knew that there was no point in begging. He knew now that the lion could never survive on his own in the wild, that he would have to go with the Frenchman. There was nothing else for it.

That night as they lay in the dark together side by side, Bertie made him a last promise. "I will find you," he whispered. "Always remember that I will find you. I promise I will."

The next morning the Frenchman shook hands with Bertie on the veranda and said goodbye. "He'll be fine, don't you worry. And one day you must come to France and see my circus, *Le Cirque Merlot*. It is the best circus in all of France." Then they left, the white lion in a wooden crate rocking from side to side in the back of the Frenchman's wagon. Bertie watched until the wagon disappeared from view.

A few months later, Bertie found himself on a ship steaming out of Cape Town, bound for England and school and a new life. As the last of Table Mountain vanished in a heat haze, he said goodbye to Africa and was not at all unhappy. He had his mother with him, for the time being at least. And after all, England was nearer France than Africa was, much nearer.

Strawbridge

The old lady drank her tea and wrinkled her nose in disgust. "I'm always doing that," she said. "I'm always letting my tea go cold." The dog scratched his ear, groaning with the pleasure of it, but eyeing me all the time.

"Is that the end then?" I asked.

She laughed and put down her cup. "I should say not," she said. And then she went on, picking a tea leaf off the tip of her tongue. "Up till now it's been just Bertie's story. He told it to me so often that I almost feel I was there when it happened. But from now on it's my story too."

"What about the white lion?" I had to know. "Did he find the white lion? Did he keep his promise?"

The old lady seemed suddenly clouded with sadness. "You must remember," she said, putting a bony hand on mine, "that true stories do not always end just as we would wish them to. Would you like to hear the truth of what happened, or shall I make something up for you just to keep you happy?"

“I want to know what really happened,” I replied.

“Then you shall,” she said. She turned from me and looked out of the window again at the butterfly lion, still blue and shimmering on the hillside.

****

Whilst Bertie was growing up on his farm in Africa with his fence all around, I was growing up here at Strawbridge in this echoing cold cavern of a house with its deer park and its high wall all around. And I grew up, for the most part, alone. I too was an only child. My mother had died giving birth to me, and Father was rarely at home. Maybe that was why the two of us, Bertie and I, got on so well from the first moment we met. We had so much in common from the very start.

Like Bertie, I scarcely ever left the confines of my home, so I had few friends.

I didn't go to school either, not to start with. I had a governess instead, Miss Tulips – everyone called her "Nolips" because she was so thin-lipped and severe. She moved around the house like a cold shadow. She lived on the top floor, like Cook, and like Nanny. Nanny Mason – bless her heart – brought me up and taught me all the do's and don'ts of life like all good nannies should. But she was more than just a nanny to me, she was a mother to me, and a wonderful one too, the best I could have had, the best anyone could have had.

My mornings were always spent at my studies with Nolips, but all the while I was looking forward to my afternoons out walking with Nanny Mason – except on Sundays,

when I was allowed to be on my own all day, if Father wasn't home for the weekend, which he usually wasn't. Then I could fly my kites when it was fine, and read my books when it wasn't. I loved my books – *Black Beauty, Little Women, Heidi* – I loved them all, because they took me outside the park walls, they took me all over the world. I met the best friends I ever had in those books – until I met Bertie, that is.

I remember it was just after my tenth birthday. It was Sunday and I was out flying my kites. But there wasn't much wind, and no matter how hard I ran, I just couldn't get even my best box kite to catch the wind and fly. I climbed all the way up Wood Hill, looking for wind. And there at the top I found it at last, enough to send my kite soaring. But then the wind gusted and my kite swirled away crazily towards the trees. I couldn't haul it in in time. It caught on a branch and stuck fast in a high elm tree in amongst the rookery. The rooks flew out cawing in protest whilst I tugged at my line, crying in my fury and frustration. I gave up, sat down and howled. That was when I noticed a boy emerging from the shadow of the trees.

"I'll get it down for you," he said, and began to climb the tree. Easy as you like, he crawled along the branch, reached out and released my kite. It floated down and landed at my feet. My best kite was torn and battered, but at least I had it back. Then he was down the tree and standing there in front of me.

"Who are you? What do you want?" I asked.

"I can mend it, if you like," he said.

"Who are you?" I asked again.

"Bertie Andrews," he replied. He was wearing a grey school uniform, and one I recognised at once. From the lion gateway I had often watched them on their walks, two by two, blue school caps, blue socks.

"You're from the school up the road, aren't you?" I said.

"You won't tell on me, will you?" His eyes were wide with sudden alarm. I saw then that his legs were scratched and bleeding.

"Been in the wars, have you?" I said.

"I've run away," he went on. "And I'm not going back, not ever."

"Where are you going?" I asked him.

He shook his head. "I don't know. In the holidays I live at my Auntie's in Salisbury, but I don't like it there."

"Haven't you got a proper home?" I said.

" 'Course I have," he replied. "Everyone has. But it's in Africa."

That whole afternoon we sat together on Wood Hill and he told me all about Africa, about his farm, about his waterhole, about his white lion and how he was somewhere in France now, in a circus and how he couldn't bear to think about him. "But I'll find him," he said fiercely. "I'll find him somehow."

To be honest, I wasn't sure how much I really believed all this about a white lion. I just didn't think lions could be white.

"But the trouble is," he went on, "even when I do find him, I won't be able to take him home to Africa like I always wanted to."

"Why not?" I asked.

"Because my mother died." He looked down and pulled at the grass beside him. "She had malaria, but I think she really died of a broken heart." When he looked up his eyes were swimming with tears. "You can, you know. Then my father sold the farm and married someone else. I never want to go back. I never want to see him again, never."

I wanted to say how sorry I was about his mother, but I couldn't find the right words to say it.

"You really live here, do you?" he said. "In that big place? It's as big as my school."

I told him then what little there was to know of me, all about Father being away in London so much, about Nolips and Nanny Mason. He sucked at the purple clover as I talked; and when neither of us had anything more to say we lay back in the sun and watched a pair of mewing buzzards wheeling overhead. I was wondering what would happen to him if he got caught.

"What are you going to do?" I said at last. "Won't you get into trouble?"

"Only if they catch me."

"But they will, they're bound to, in the end," I said. "You've got to go back, before they miss you."

After a while he propped himself up on his elbow and looked down at me.

"Maybe you're right," he said. "Maybe they won't have missed me yet. Maybe it's not too late. But if I go back, could I come again? I can face it if I can come again. Would you let me? I'll mend your kite, really I will." And he gave me a smile so melting that I couldn't refuse him.

So it was arranged. He would meet me under the big wych elm on Wood Hill every Sunday afternoon at three, or as close to three as he could. He would have to come through the woods so that he could never be seen from the house. I knew full well that if Nolips ever found out, there'd be merry hell to pay – for both of us, probably. Bertie shrugged, and said that if he got caught, all they could do at school was beat him, and that once more wouldn't make much difference anyway. And if they expelled him, well then, that would suit him fine.

And All's Well

Bertie came every Sunday after that. Sometimes it couldn't be for long because he had detention back at school, or maybe I'd have to send him away because Father was down for the weekend, shooting pheasants in the park with his friends. We had to be careful. He *did* mend my best box kite, but after a while we forgot all about flying kites, and we just talked and walked.

Bertie and I lived for our Sundays. In those next two years we became, first, good companions, and then best of friends. We never told each other we were, because we didn't need to. The more I got to know him, the more I believed everything about Africa, and about "The White Prince" in the circus somewhere in France. I believed him too when he told me again and again how somehow, someday he would find his white lion, and make sure that he'd never have to live behind bars again.

The school holidays always dragged interminably because Bertie wasn't there on Sundays. But at least there were no lessons to endure with Nolips. She always went off in the holidays to stay with her sister by the sea in Margate. Instead of her lessons though, Nanny Mason would take me on endless nature walks – "walks on the wild side", she called them.

I grumbled and stamped my feet. "But it's so boring," I'd tell her. "If we had zebras and water buffaloes and elephants and baboons and giraffes and wildebeests and spotted hyenas and black mamba snakes and vultures and lions, I wouldn't mind. But a few deer, a fox's hole, and maybe a badger's set? A dozen rabbit droppings, one robin's nest and some cuckoo pint?" Once, before I could stop myself, I said: "And do you know, Nanny, there's white lions in Africa, real white lions?"

"Fancy that," she laughed. "You and your fairy tales, Millie. You read too many books."

Bertie and I didn't dare write letters to each other in case someone found them and read them. But school term came round again and he'd be there under the wych elm on the first Sunday at three o'clock without fail. What we found to talk about all the time I cannot honestly remember. He sometimes said how he could never look at a circus poster without thinking of "The White Prince". But as time passed, he talked less and less of the white lion, and then not at all. I thought that maybe he had forgotten all about him.

We both grew up too quickly. We had one last summer term together, before I was to be sent off to a convent school by the sea in Sussex, and he was to go away to a college under the shadow of Canterbury Cathedral. We treasured each meeting, knowing how few we had left. We were silent in our sadness. The love between us stayed unspoken. We knew it when our eyes met, when our hands touched. We were just so sure of each other. Before he left me that last Sunday he gave me a kite he had made in carpentry lessons at school and told me I had to think of him every time I flew it.

Then he went his way to his college and I went mine to my convent, and we didn't see each other again. I was always very careful where I flew the kite he'd given me, just in case I lost it up a tree and couldn't get it back again. I thought that if I lost the kite it would be like losing Bertie for ever. I kept it on top of my cupboard in my bedroom. It's still up there to this day.

Now we did write because we were away from home and it was safe to do so. We wrote letters that talked to each other just as we had done all those years on Wood Hill. My letters were long and rambling, about tittle-tattle at school, about how much happier it was at home now that Nolips had left. His were always short and his handwriting so tiny you could hardly read it. He was no happier shut inside the walls of his cathedral precinct than he had been before. There were bells, he wrote, always bells – bells to wake you up, bells for meals, bells for lessons, bells, bells, bells cutting his days into thin slices. How we both hated bells. The last thing he heard at night was the nightwatchman walking the city walls outside his dormitory window, ringing his bell and calling out: "Twelve o'clock. A fine night. And all's well." But he knew, as I knew, as everyone knew, that all was not well, that a great war was coming. His letters, and mine, were full of the dread of it.

Then the storm of war broke. Like many storms, it rumbled only distantly at first, and we all hoped it would somehow pass us by. But it was not to be like that. Father looked so grand in his khaki uniform and shiny brown boots. He said goodbye to Nanny Mason and me on the front steps, climbed into his car and was driven away. We never saw him again. I can't pretend I grieved much when the news came that he had been killed. I know a daughter should grieve for a dead father, and I tried to. I was sad of course, but it is difficult to grieve for someone you never really knew, and my father had always been a stranger to me. Worse, so much worse for me, was the thought that the same thing might one day happen to Bertie.

I just hoped and prayed that the war would end whilst he was still safe at college in Canterbury. Nanny Mason kept saying it would all be over by Christmas. But Christmas came each year and it never was over.

I remember Bertie's last letter from college by heart.

Dearest Millie,

I am old enough now to join up, so I shall. I have had all I can take of fences and walls and bells. I want to fly free, and this seems to be the only way I can do it. Besides, they need men. I can see you smiling at that. All you remember is a boy. I am over six foot now, and I shave twice a week. Honestly! I may not write again for some time, but whatever happens I shall be thinking of you always.

Your

Bertie

And that was the last I was to hear of him – for a while, at least.

A Lot of Old Codswallop

The dog was whining at the kitchen door. "Let Jack out for me, will you?" said the old lady. "There's a dear. I'll tell you what, I'll fetch down the kite Bertie made for me, shall I? You'd like to see it, wouldn't you?" And she went out.

I was only too happy to let the dog out and shut the door on him.

She was back sooner than I expected. "There," she said, setting the kite down on the table in front of me. "What do you think of it then?" It was huge, much bigger than I had expected, and covered in dust. It was made of brown canvas stretched over a wooden frame. All the kites I had seen had been more colourful, more flamboyant. I think the disappointment must have shown in my face.

"She still flies, you know," she said, blowing the dust off. "You should see how she goes. You should see her." She sat down in her chair and I waited for her to begin again. "Now then, where was I?" she asked. "I'm so forgetful these days."

"Bertie's last letter," I said. "He was just going off to the war. But what about the white lion, 'The White Prince'? What happened to him?" I could hear the dog barking wildly outside. She smiled at me. "Everything comes to he who waits," she said. "Why don't you have a look out of the window?"

I looked. The lion on the hillside was blue no more. It was white now, and the dog was bounding across the hillside, chasing away a cloud of blue butterflies that rose all around him. "He chases everything that moves," she said. "But don't worry. He won't catch a single one. He never catches anything."

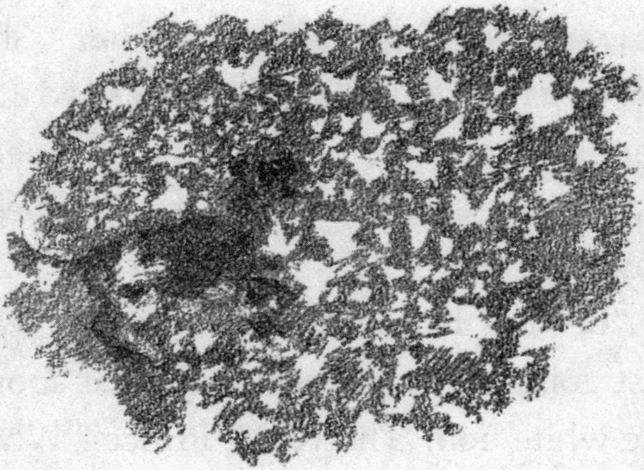

"Not *that* lion," I said. "I meant the lion in the story. What happened to him?"

"Don't you see? They're the same. The lion out there on the hillside and the lion in the story. They're the same."

"I don't understand," I said.

"You soon will," she replied. "You soon will." She took a deep breath before she began again.

****

For many years Bertie never spoke about the fighting in the trenches. He always said it was a nightmare best forgotten, best kept to himself. But later on when he'd had time to reflect, when time had done its healing perhaps, then he told me something of how it had been.

At seventeen, he'd found himself marching with his regiment along the straight roads of northern France up to the front line, heads and hearts high with hope and expectation. Within a few months he was sitting huddled at the bottom of a muddy trench, hands over his head, head between his knees, curling himself into himself as tight as he would go, sick with terror as the shells and whizzbangs blew the world apart around him. Then the whistle would blow and they'd be out and over the top into No Man's Land, bayonets fixed and walking towards the German trenches into the ratatat of machine-gun fire. To the left of him and to the right of him his friends would fall, and he would walk on, waiting for the bullet with his name on which he knew could cut him down at any moment.

At dawn they always had to come out of their dugouts and "stand to" in the trenches, just in case there was an attack. The Germans often attacked at dawn. That's how it was on the morning of his twentieth birthday. They came swarming over No Man's Land out of the early morning sun, but they were soon spotted and mown down like so much ripe corn. Then they were turning and running. The whistle went, and Bertie led his men over the top to counter-attack. But as always the Germans were expecting them, and the usual slaughter began. Bertie was hit in the leg and fell into a shellhole. He thought of waiting there all day and then crawling back under cover of darkness, but his wound was bleeding badly and he could not staunch it. He decided he had to try to crawl back to the trenches whilst he still had the strength to do it.

Hugging the ground, he was almost at the wire, almost back to safety, when he heard someone crying out in No Man's Land. It was a cry he could not ignore. He found two of his men lying side by side, and so badly wounded that they could not move. One of them was already unconscious. He hoisted him onto his shoulders and made for the trenches, the bullets whipping and whining around him. The man was heavy and Bertie fell several times under his weight, but he got himself to his feet again and staggered on,

until they tumbled together down into the trench. The stretcher-bearers tried to take Bertie away. He'd bleed to death, they said. But he would not listen. One of his own men was still lying wounded out there in No Man's Land, and he was going to bring him in, no matter what.

Waving his hands above his head, Bertie climbed out of the trench and walked forward. The firing stopped almost at once. He was so weak himself by now that he could scarcely walk, but he managed to reach the wounded man and drag him back. They say that in the end both sides, German and British, were up on the parapets and cheering him on as he stumbled back towards his lines. Then other men were running out to help him and after that he didn't know any more.

When he woke up he found himself in hospital lying in a bed, with the two friends he had rescued on either side.

He was still there some weeks later when he was told that he was to be awarded the Victoria Cross for his bravery under fire. He was the hero of the hour, the pride of his regiment.

Afterwards Bertie always called it a "lot of old codswallop". To be really brave, he said, you have to overcome fear. You have to be frightened in the first place, and he hadn't been. There wasn't time to be frightened. He did what he did without thinking, just as he had saved the white lion cub all those years before when he was a boy in Africa. Of course, they made a great fuss of him in the hospital, and he loved all that, but his leg did not heal as well as it should have. He was still there in the hospital when I found him.

It was not entirely by accident that I found him. For over three years now there had been no letter, no word from him at all. He had warned me, I know, but the long silence was hard to bear. Every time the postman came, I hoped, and the pang of disappointment was sharper each time there was no letter from him. I told all to Nanny Mason who dried my tears and told me to pray, and that she would too. She was sure there'd be a letter soon.

Without Nanny I don't know how I would have gone on living. I was so miserable. I had seen the wounded men coming back from France, blinded, gassed, crippled, and always dreaded seeing

Bertie's face amongst them. I had seen the long lists in the newspapers of all the men who had been killed or who were "missing". I looked each day for his name and thanked God every time I did not find it. But still he never wrote, and I had to know why. I thought maybe he had been so badly wounded that he could not write, that he was lying in some hospital alone and unloved. So I determined I would become a nurse. I would go to France, and heal and comfort as best I could, and just hope that somehow I might find him. But I soon discovered that amongst so many men in uniform it would be hopeless to go looking for him. I did not even know his regiment, nor his rank. I had no idea where to begin.

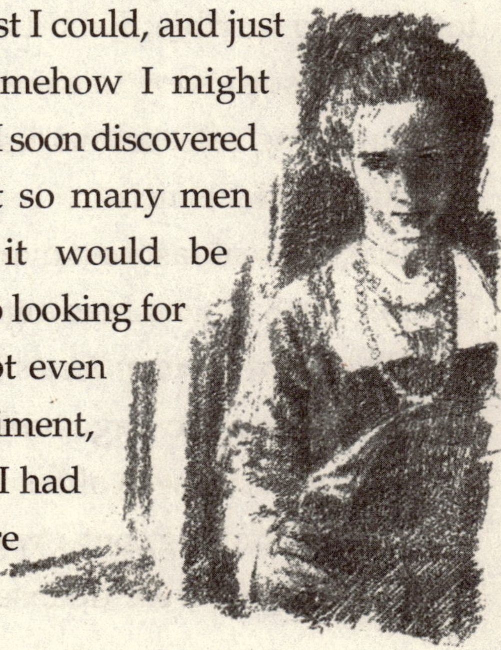

I was sent to a hospital some fifty miles behind the lines, not too far from Amiens. The hospital was a converted chateau with turrets and great wide staircases, and chandeliers in the wards. But it was so cold in winter that many of the men died as much from the cold as from their wounds. We did all we could for them, but we were short of doctors and short of medicines. There were always so many men coming in, and their wounds were terrible, so terrible. Each time we saved one it was such a joy to us. In the midst of the suffering all around us, we needed some joy, believe me.

I was at breakfast one morning – it was June of 1918. I was reading a magazine, the *Illustrated London News*, I remember, when I turned the page and saw a face I knew at once. He was older, thinner in the face and unsmiling, but I was sure it was Bertie. His eyes were deepset and gentle, just as I remembered them. And there was his name: "Captain Albert Andrews VC". There was a whole article underneath about what he had done, and how he was still recovering from his wounds in a hospital, a hospital that turned out to be little more than ten miles away. Wild horses would not have kept me from him. The next Sunday I cycled over.

He was sleeping when I saw him first, propped up on his pillows, one hand behind his head. "Hello," I said.

He opened his eyes and frowned at me. It was a moment or two before he knew me.

"Been in the wars, have you?" I said.

"Something like that," he replied.

The White Prince

They said I could take him out in his wheelchair every Sunday so long as I didn't tire him, so long as he was back by supper. As Bertie said, it was just like our Sundays had been when we were little. There was only one place we could go to, a small village only a mile away. There wasn't much left of the village, a few streets of battered houses, a church with its steeple broken off halfway up, and a café in the square, thankfully still intact. I would push him in his chair some of the way and he would hobble along with his stick when he felt strong enough. Mostly we would sit in the café and talk, or walk along the river and talk. We had so many years to catch up on.

He hadn't written, he told me, because he'd thought that each day at the front might be his last, that he might be dead by sunset. So many of his friends were dead. Sooner or later, it had to be his turn. He wanted me to forget him, so that I wouldn't know when he was killed, so that I wouldn't be hurt. What you don't know, you don't grieve over, he said. He had never imagined that he would survive, that he would ever see me again.

It was on one of our Sunday outings that I noticed the poster across the street on the wall of what was left of the post office. The colours were faded and the bottom half had been torn away, but at the top the print was quite clear. It was in French. *Cirque Merlot*, it read, and underneath: *Le Prince Blanc* – The White

Prince! And just discernible, a picture of a lion roaring, a white lion. Bertie had seen it too.

"It's him!" he breathed. "It has to be him!" With no help from me, he was out of his wheelchair, stick in hand, limping across the street towards the café.

The café owner was wiping down the tables outside on the pavement. "The circus," Bertie began, pointing back at the poster. He didn't speak much French, so he shouted in English instead. "You know, lions, elephants, clowns!"

The man looked at him blankly and shrugged. So Bertie started roaring like a lion and clawing the air. I could see alarmed faces at the window of the café, and the man was backing away shaking his head. I ripped the poster off the wall and brought it over. My French was a little better than Bertie's. The café owner understood at once.

"Ah," he said, smiling with relief. "Monsieur Merlot. *Le cirque. C'est triste, très triste.*" And he went on in broken English: "The circus. He is finished. Sad, very sad. The soldiers, you understand, they want beer and wine, and girls maybe.

They do not want the circus. No one comes, and so Monsieur Merlot, he have to close the circus. But what can he do with all the animals? He keep them. He feed them.

But the shells come, more and more they come, and his house – how you say it? – it is bombarded. Many animals are dead. But Monsieur Merlot, he stay. He keep only the elephants, the monkeys, and the lion, 'The White Prince'. Everyone love The White Prince. The army, they take all the hay for the horses. There is no food for the animals. So Monsieur Merlot, he take his gun and he have to shoot them. No more circus. Finish. *Triste, très triste.*"

"All of them?" cried Bertie. "He shot all of them?"

"No," said the man. "Not all. He keep The White Prince. He could not shoot The White Prince, never. Monsieur Merlot, he bring him from Africa many years ago. Most famous lion in all of France. He love the lion like a son. That lion, he make Monsieur Merlot a rich man. But he is not rich no more. He lose everything. Now he have nothing, just The White

Prince. It is true. I think they die together. Maybe they die already. Who knows?"

"This Monsieur Merlot," Bertie said, "where does he live? Where can I find him?"

The man pointed out of the village. "Seven, maybe eight kilometres," he said. "It is an old house by the river. Over the bridge and on the left. Not too far. But maybe Monsieur Merlot he is not there no more. Maybe the house is not there no more. Who knows?" And with a last shrug he turned and went indoors.

There were always army lorries rumbling through the village, so it was not at all difficult to hitch a ride. We left the wheelchair behind in the café. Bertie said it would only get in the way, that he could manage well enough with his stick. We found the house, a mill house, just over the bridge where the café owner had said it would be. There wasn't much left of it. The barns all around were shell-blasted, the ruins blackened by fire. Only the main house still had a roof, but it too had not gone unscathed. One corner of the building had been holed and was partially covered by canvas that flapped in the wind. There was no sign of life.

Bertie knocked on the door several times, but there was no answer. The place frightened me. I wanted to leave at once, but Bertie would not hear of it. When he pushed gently at the door, it opened. Everything was dark inside. I did not want to go in, but Bertie took me firmly by the hand.

"He's in here," he whispered. "I can smell him."

And it was true. There was a smell in the air, pungent and rank, and to me quite unfamiliar.

"*Qui est là*?" said a voice from the darkness of the room. "*Qu'est-ce que vous voulez*?" He spoke so quietly you could hardly hear him over the rush of the river outside. I could just make out a large bed under the window at the far end of the room. A man was lying there, propped up on a pile of cushions.

"Monsieur Merlot?" Bertie asked.

"*Oui*?"

As we walked forward together, Bertie went on: "I am Bertie Andrews. Many years ago you came to my farm in Africa, and you bought a white lion cub. Do you still have him?"

As if in answer the white blanket at the end of the bed became a lion, rose from the bed, sprang down and was padding towards us, a terrible rumble in his throat. I froze where I was as the lion came right up to us.

"It's all right, Millie. He won't hurt us," said Bertie, putting an arm round me. "We're old friends." Moaning and yowling, the lion rubbed himself up against Bertie so hard that we had to hold on to each other to stop ourselves from falling over.

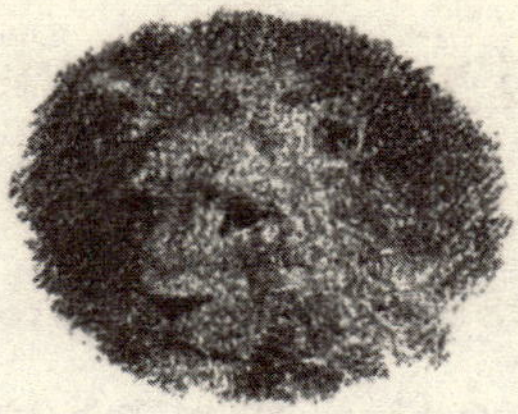

A Miracle, A Miracle!

The lion eyed Bertie for a few moments. The yowling stopped, and he began to grunt and groan with pleasure as Bertie smoothed his mane and scratched him between the eyes. "Remember me?" he said to the lion. "Remember Africa?"

"You are the one? I am not dreaming this?" said Monsieur Merlot. "You are the boy in Africa, the one who tried to set him free?"

"I've grown a bit," said Bertie, "but it's me." Bertie and Monsieur Merlot shook hands warmly, while the lion turned his attention on me, licking my hand with his rough warm tongue. I just gritted my teeth and hoped he wouldn't eat it.

"I did all I could," Monsieur Merlot said, shaking his head. "But look at him now. Just skins and bones like me. All my animals they are gone, except *Le Prince Blanc*. He is all I have left. I had to shoot my elephants, you know that? I had to. What else could I do? There was no food to feed them. I could not let them starve, could I?"

Bertie sat down on the bed, put his arms around the lion's neck and buried his head in his mane. The lion rubbed up against him, but he kept looking at me. I kept my distance, I can tell you. I just could not get it out of my head that lions do *eat* people, particularly if they are hungry lions. And this lion was very hungry indeed. You could see his ribs, and his hip bones too.

"Don't worry, *monsieur*," said Bertie. "I will find you food. I will find food enough for both of you. I promise."

The driver of the ambulance I waved down thought at first that he was just giving a nurse a lift back to the village. He was, as you can imagine, a little more reluctant when he saw the old man, and then Bertie, and still more when he saw a huge white lion.

The driver swallowed a lot, said nothing all the way, and just nodded when Bertie asked him to let us out in the village square. And so there we were half an hour or so later, the four of us sitting outside the café in the sun, the lion at our feet gnawing a huge bone the butcher was only too pleased to sell us. Monsieur Merlot ate a plate of fried potatoes in complete silence and washed it down with a bottle of red wine. Around us gathered an astonished crowd of villagers, of French soldiers, of British soldiers – at a safe distance. All the while Bertie scratched the lion's head right between his eyes.

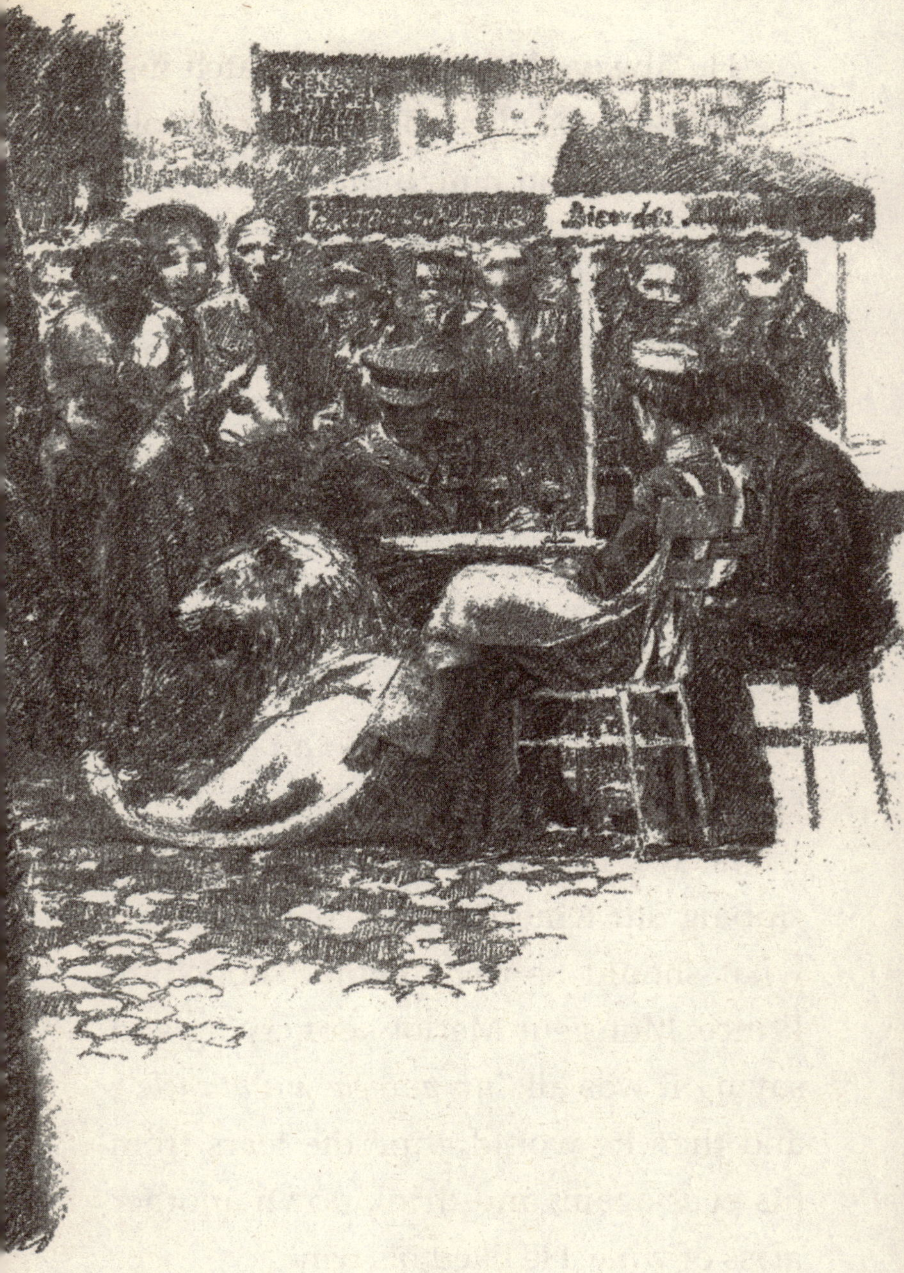

"He always liked a good scratch just there," Bertie said, smiling at me. "I told you I would find him, didn't I?" he went on. "I was never sure you really believed me."

"Well, I did," I replied, and then I added: "After a while, anyway." It was the truth. I suppose that may explain why I took all that happened that morning so much in my stride. It was amazing, surreal almost, but it was no surprise. A prophecy come true, like a wish come true – and this was both – can never be entirely surprising.

As we sat there outside the café sipping our wine, the three of us decided what should be done about The White Prince. Monsieur Merlot kept crying and saying it was all "*un miracle, un miracle*"; and then he would wipe the tears from his eyes again, and drink down another glass of wine. He liked his wine.

The whole plan was entirely Bertie's idea. To be honest, I didn't see how it could possibly be done. I should have known better. I should have known that once Bertie had set his heart on something, he would see it through.

As we walked the lion down the village street, Bertie leaning on the lion, me pushing Monsieur Merlot in the wheelchair, the crowd parted in front of us and backed away. Then they began to follow us, at a discreet distance, of course, up the road towards Bertie's hospital. Someone must have gone on ahead to warn them, because we could now see a huddle of doctors and nurses gathered on the front steps, and there were people peering out of every window. As we came up to the hospital, an officer stepped forward, a colonel it was.

Bertie saluted. "Sir," he began, "Monsieur Merlot here is a very old friend of mine. He will need a bed in the hospital.

He's in need of rest, sir, and a lot of good food. The same goes for the lion. So I wondered, sir, if you'd mind if we used the walled garden behind the hospital. There's a shed in there where the lion could sleep. He'd be quite safe, and so would we. I know him. He doesn't eat people. Monsieur Merlot here has said that if I can feed the lion and take care of him, then I can take him back to England with me."

"The brass cheek of it!" the colonel spluttered as he came down the steps. "Who the devil do you think you are anyway?" he said. And that was when he recognised Bertie. "You're the fellow that won the VC, aren't you?" he said, suddenly a lot more polite. "Andrews, isn't it?"

"Yes, sir, and I want to take the lion back to England when I go. We've got somewhere in mind for him to live," and he turned to me. "Haven't we?" he said.

"Yes," I said.

It wasn't at all easy persuading the colonel to agree. He began to soften only when we told him that if we didn't look after the white lion, no one else would, and then he would have to be taken away and shot. A lion, the symbol of Britain, shot! Not at all good for morale, Bertie argued. And the colonel listened.

It wasn't any easier persuading the powers that be in England to allow the lion to come back home when the war was over, but somehow Bertie managed it. He just wouldn't take no for an answer. Bertie always said afterwards that it was the medal that did it, that without the prestige of the Victoria Cross behind him he'd never have got away with it, and The White Prince would never have come home.

When we docked at Dover, the band was playing and the bunting was out, and there were photographers and newspaper reporters everywhere. The White Prince walked off the ship at Bertie's side to a hero's welcome. "The British Lion Comes Home" roared the newspapers the next day.

So we came back here to Strawbridge, Bertie, The White Prince and me. I married Bertie in the village church. I remember, Bertie had a bit of a disagreement with the vicar because he wouldn't allow the lion inside the church for the wedding. I was very glad he didn't – but I never told Bertie that. Nanny Mason adored both Bertie and The White Prince, but she insisted on washing him often, because he smelt – the lion, not Bertie. Nanny Mason stayed on with the three of us – "her three children", she called us – until she retired to the seaside in Devon.

The Butterfly Lion

We never had children of our own – just The White Prince – and I can tell you, he was enough of a family for anyone. He roamed free in the park just as we had planned he would, and chased the deer and the rabbits whenever he felt like it; but he never did learn how to kill for himself. You can't teach old lions new tricks. He lived well, on venison mostly, and slept on a sofa on the landing – I wouldn't have him inside our bedroom, no matter how often Bertie asked. You have to draw the line somewhere.

Bertie's leg never recovered completely. When it was bad, he often needed a stick, or me, or the lion to lean on. It pained him a lot, particularly when the weather was cold and damp, and he never slept well. On Sundays the three of us would wander the park together, and he would sit on the top of Wood Hill with his arm around his old friend's neck and I would fly kites. As you know, I've always loved kites; and so, it turned out, did the lion, who pounced on several of them as they landed, savaged them and ripped them to pieces.

The lion never showed any interest in escaping, and even if he'd wanted to, the park wall was too high for an old lion to jump. Wherever Bertie went he wanted to go too. And if ever Bertie went out in the car, then he'd sit by me near the stove in the kitchen, and watch me with those great amber eyes, listening all the while for the sound of Bertie's car coming up the gravel to the front of the house.

The old lion lived on into a ripe old age. But he became stiff in his legs and could see very little towards the end. He spent his last days stretched out asleep at Bertie's feet, right where you're sitting now. When he died, we buried him at the bottom of the hill out there. Bertie wanted it that way so he could always see the spot from the kitchen window. I suggested we plant a tree in case we forgot where he was. "I'll never forget," he said fiercely. "Never. And besides, he deserves a lot more than a tree."

Bertie grieved on for weeks, months after the lion died. There was nothing I could do to cheer him or even console him. He would sit for hours in his room, or go off on long walks all on his own. He seemed so shut away inside himself, so distant. Try as I did, I could not reach him.

Then one day I was in the kitchen here, when I saw him hurrying down the hill, waving his stick and shouting for me.

"I've got it," he cried, as he came in, "I've got it at last." He showed me the end of his stick. It was white. "See that, Millie? Chalk! It's chalk underneath, isn't it?"

"So?" I said.

"You know the famous White Horse on the hillside at Uffington, the one they carved out of the chalk a thousand years ago? That horse never died, did it? It's still alive, isn't it? Well, that's what we're going to do, so he'll never be forgotten.

We'll carve The White Prince out on the hillside – he'll be there for ever, and he'll be white for ever too."

"It'll take a bit of time, won't it?" I said.

"We've got plenty, haven't we?" he replied, with the same smile he had smiled at me when he was a ten-year-old boy asking me if he could come back and mend my kite for me.

It took the next twenty years to do it. Every spare hour we had, we were up there scraping away with spades and trowels; and we had buckets and wheelbarrows to carry away the turf and the earth. It was hard, back-breaking work, but it was a labour of love. We did it, Bertie and I, we did it together – paws, claws, tail, mane, until he was whole and perfect in every detail.

It was just after we'd finished that the butterflies first came. We noticed that when the sun comes out after the rain in the summer, the butterflies – Adonis Blues, they are, I looked them up – come out to drink on the chalk face. Then The White Prince becomes a butterfly lion, and breathes again like a living creature.

So now you know how Bertie's white lion became The White Prince and how The White Prince became our butterfly lion.

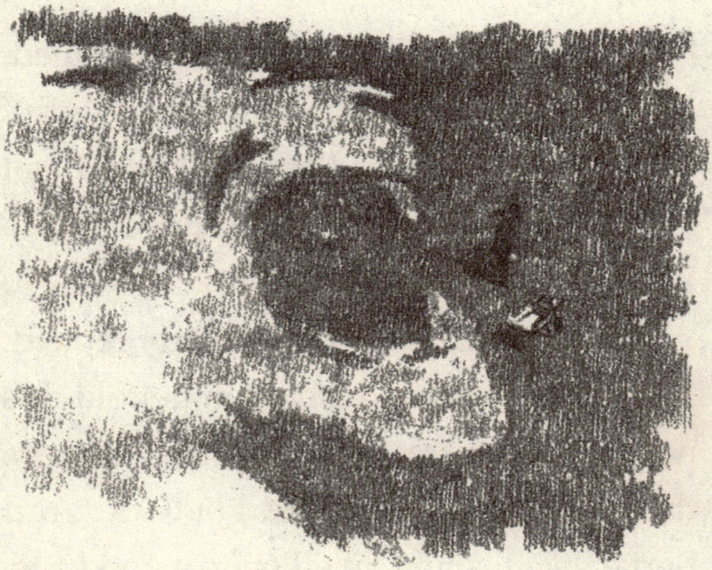

And the Lion Shall Lie Down with the Lamb

The old lady turned to me and smiled. "There," she said. "That's my story."

"And what about Bertie?" I knew as I asked that I shouldn't have. But I had to know.

"He's dead, dear," the old lady replied. "It's what happens when you get old. It's nothing to worry about. It's lonely, though. That's why I've got Jack. And Bertie, like his lion, lived on to a good age. He's buried out there under the hill beside The White Prince." She looked back at the hill for a moment. "And that's where I belong too," she said.

She tapped the table with her fingers. "Come on. Time to go. Back to school with you before they miss you and you get yourself into trouble. We wouldn't want that, would we?" She laughed. "Do you know, that's just what I told Bertie all those years ago when he ran away from school. You remember?" She was on her feet now. "Come on, I'll drive you. And don't look so worried. I'll make sure no one sees you. It'll be like you've never been gone."

"Can I come again?" I asked.

" 'Course you can," she said. "I may not always be easy to find, but I'll be here. I'll just tidy away the tea things, and then we'll go, shall we?"

It was a very old-fashioned car, black and upright and dignified, with a leathery smell and a whiny engine.

She dropped me at the bottom of the school park, by the fence.

"Take care, dear," she said. "And be sure you come again soon, won't you? I'll be expecting you."

"I will," I replied. I climbed the fence before I turned to wave; but by that time the car had gone.

To my huge relief no one had missed me. And best of all, Basher Beaumont was in the sickroom. He'd gone down with measles. I just hoped his measles would last a long time, a very long time.

All through supper I could think of nothing but Bertie Andrews and his white lion. Stew and dumplings and then semolina pudding with raspberry jam – again! It was as I was picking my way through my slimy semolina that I remembered Bertie Andrews had been at this school. Maybe, I thought, maybe he'd had to sit here and eat slimy semolina just as we did now.

I looked up at the honours boards around the dining hall, at the names of all the boys who had won scholarships over the years. I looked for Bertie Andrews. He wasn't there. But then, I thought, why should he be? Maybe, like me, he wasn't brilliant at his school work. Not everyone wins scholarships.

Cookie – Mr Cook, my history teacher – was sitting beside me at the end of my table. "Who were you looking for, Morpurgo?" he asked suddenly.

"Andrews, sir," I said. "Bertie Andrews."

"Andrews? Andrews? There's an Albert Andrews who won the Victoria Cross in the First World War. You mean him?" Cookie scraped his bowl clean and licked the back of his spoon. "I love raspberry jam. You'll find his name in the chapel, under the East Window, under the War memorial. But he wasn't killed in the war, you know. He lived down at Strawbridge, that place with the lion on the gateway, just across the main road. He died, maybe ten, twelve years ago, soon after I came to teach here. The only old boy ever to win the VC. That's why they put up a memorial plaque to him in the chapel after he died. I remember the day his wife came to unveil it – his widow, I should say. Poor dear, just herself and her dog in that great big place. She died only a few months later. Broken heart, they say. You can, you know. You can die of a broken heart.

That house has been empty ever since. No family to take it on. No one wants it. Too big, you see. Shame."

I said I wanted to be excused, to go to the toilet. I hurtled down the passage, out across the courtyard and into the chapel. The small brass plaque was exactly where Cookie had said it was, but hidden by a vase of flowers. I moved the vase to one side. The plaque read:

> ALBERT ANDREWS VC
> BORN 1897. DIED 1968.
> AN OLD BOY OF THIS SCHOOL.
> AND THE LION SHALL LIE DOWN
> WITH THE LAMB.

All night long I tried to puzzle it out. Cookie was wrong. He just had to be. I never slept a wink.

Adonis Blues

The next afternoon after games were over, I went over the fence at the bottom of the park, hared up through Innocents Breach, across the road, along the wall and slipped through the iron gateway with the stone lion roaring above me. It was raining a light summer rain.

I tried knocking at the front door. No one came. No dog barked. I went round to the back and peered in through the kitchen window. The box kite was still there on the kitchen table, but there was no sign of the old lady anywhere. I rattled the kitchen door, and knocked louder, again and again. I called out: "Hello!

Hello!" There was no reply. I banged on the window. "Are you there? Are you there?"

"We all are," came a voice from behind me. I turned. There was no one there. I was alone, alone with the white lion on the hillside. I had imagined it.

I climbed the hill and went to sit in the grass above the white of the lion's mane. I looked down at the great house beneath me. Jackdaws cawed overhead. There was bracken and grass growing out of the gutters and around the chimney pots. Some of the windows were boarded up. Drainpipes hung loose and rusting. The place was empty, quite empty.

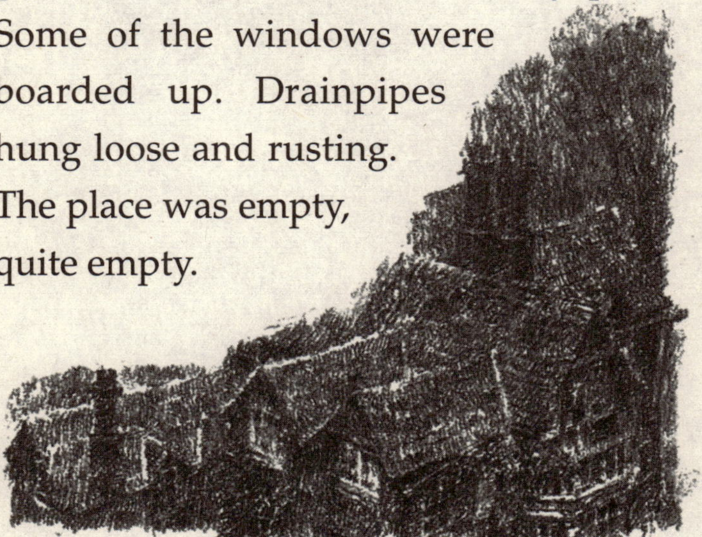

The rain suddenly stopped and the sun warmed the back of my neck. The first butterfly landed on my arm. It was blue. "Adonis Blues, Adonis Blues," came the voice again, like an echo in my head. Then the sky around me was filled with butterflies, and they were settling to drink on the chalk.

"Adonis Blues, remember?" The same voice, a real voice, her voice. And this time I knew it was not in my head. "Keep him white for us, there's a dear. We don't want him forgotten, you see. And think of us sometimes, won't you?"

"I will," I cried. "I will."

And I swear I felt the earth tremble beneath me with the roar of a distant lion.